THE GOLDEN LOOM

PALANCA PRIZE WINNERS FOR CHILDREN

TAHANAN BOOKS FOR YOUNG READERS

MANILA

The publisher gratefully acknowledges the Carlos Palanca Foundation, without whose support this book would not have been possible.

Published by Tahanan Books for Young Readers
A division of Tahanan Pacific, Inc.
Room 203, Narra Building, 2276 Pasong Tamo Extension
Makati City, Philippines
Sales and marketing telefax: (632) 818-2482
Or email **marketing@tahananbooks.com**

Visit us on the World Wide Web at www.tahananbooks.com

Cover Illustration by Hermes Alegre
Book design by Auri Asuncion Yambao

Printed in the Philippines by Studio Graphics
4   6   8   10   9   7   5

National Library of the Philippines Cataloging-in-Publication Data

Recommended entry:

The Golden loom : Palanca prize
    winners for children. – Makati City :
    Tahanan Books for Young Readers,
    c1997.
    1v

    1. Children's literature, Philippine
(English). 2. Palanca prize - Philippines -
Awards.

PZ90P5 808.89'9282 1997 P973000005
ISBN 971-630-075-1

Contents

THE
GOLDEN
LOOM

The Dream Weavers

by Carla M. Pacis
Illustration by Hermès Alègrè

long time ago, high up in the land of the Itneg people, there lived a wizened, old woman. She had a face wrinkled like a prune by the sun and eyes that twinkled like dew on a bright, early morning. Her strong shoulders and arms bore beautiful tattoos, which, if the weather permitted, she showed off. Her tattoos wove around her arms like snakes and rested on her shoulders. These tattoos were of a geometric pattern that had been passed down from generation to generation.

She was slightly stooped from age and from her arduous chores. Each morning she walked to a nearby stream to fetch water, which she needed to cook her meals and dye her threads. Then she chopped the firewood. After her chores were done, she settled under the eaves of her hut to weave her much-loved blankets.

Her name was Bugan and she lived in a squat, wooden hut surrounded by a little vegetable garden, where she grew string beans and cabbages. Beyond, rose emerald mountains from which she drew inspiration for the patterns of the blankets she wove. Her hut, like most huts in the village, was built above the ground. Five short steps led to a small room containing a huge, stone stove, where Bugan cooked her simple meals and which kept her hut nice and warm during the cold months.

Each afternoon Bugan sat under the eaves of her house, her legs fully stretched out in front of her as she arranged her back strap carefully around her waist. She sat facing the mountains as she wove all sorts of magical creatures onto her blankets. Everyday Bugan wove until she could no longer see the threads in the failing light.

Bugan was never still when she wove. She moved back and forth, making sure the threads were taut, as she deftly threw the *baliga* in between the strings. She pushed the *gur-on* not too tightly, but just enough, to give the cloth strength. It was important that she throw the baliga just right, as this determined the pattern of the blanket. The click-clacking of Bugan's weaving was heard throughout the village, and somehow the rhythmic sound assured the villagers that all was well.

Bugan dyed her own threads with plants that grew in the forest. Every so often, she picked up her walking stick and took long hikes through the forest. She gathered the plants she knew would give her the colors she needed. Mountain apples for red, ginger root for yellow, and *duhat* berries for blue.

She squashed the berries and chopped the ginger into little pieces. Then she poured them into different vats of

boiling water. The water slowly began to turn the color of the berries. When the water was the shade she desired, she threw the raw threads into the vat and left them there until they fattened with color. The threads gleamed like exquisite jewels in the sun. As soon as they dried, Bugan separated and arranged them on the loom, according to the pattern she wished to make.

For the young maidens, Bugan wove blankets full of flowers. When they tucked themselves under these blankets, they dreamt of the handsome warrior they would one day marry and the strong and healthy children they would bear.

For the older women, she wove butterflies. They, in turn, dreamt of their daughters marrying brave warriors and their sons, dutiful wives. Bugan also filled their blankets with stars, and they dreamt of the wonderful moments in their lives and of their future with their ancestors.

For the warriors, Bugan wove animals: the deer for agility and swiftness and the horse for valor and strength. For the old men, she wove the snake or the frog, for these animals endowed wisdom. Protected by these blankets, the wise men planned the destiny of their little village.

Bugan continued to weave for her people. However, deep in her heart, she knew she would soon die. She began to prepare for her journey to the other world. She started to weave her burial blanket and search the village for another to take her place.

The village girls tried their hand at the loom, but found it too tedious. Their backs hurt and their fingers fumbled. And to have to dye the threads! It was much easier to buy blankets from the lowlanders, even if they weren't nearly as beautiful as those Bugan made. Alas! The Itneg maidens never learned to weave.

Bugan eventually joined her ancestors in Maglawa, the Itneg heaven, without finding anyone to take her place. The entire village mourned her. They wrapped her in her burial blanket and, for days, sat around her, chanting and asking their ancestors to receive her in Maglawa.

The village slowly began to change after Bugan's death. The warriors became restless and adopted the bad habits of the lowlanders. The women became lazy and neglected Itneg customs and traditions. They forgot to teach their children the wise ways of the elders. The elders were often ignored and, at times, ridiculed! But most unusual of all, everyone in the village stopped dreaming! When the villagers realized this, panic ensued. Suddenly, no one had any hopes or wishes. Everyone became bored and listless. No wonder the village had changed so much!

The village elders met and decided that something had to be done. Their village was dying! New blankets had to be woven for the dreams to come again. Warriors were sent out in search of a weaver of dreams.

The warriors were eager for adventure as none had come their way in a long time. The Itnegs no longer fought neighboring tribes for land or women. Theirs was a time of peace.

Aponitalau was the most excited of all the young men. He was anxious to prove himself. Unlike his ancestors who had wars to fight to prove their bravery, Aponitalau would have to prove his bravery in another way. When the village elders asked the warriors to search for a weaver to take

Bugan's place, Aponitalau knew he had found his adventure.

Aponitalau set out with the other warriors even before the sun first showed its rays. Each chose a different path at the end of the village road. Aponitalau chose the path to the farthest mountain.

For many days and nights, Aponitalau climbed up the mountain and crossed to others. He traversed many streams and slept in caves or under trees. He hunted in the forests or fished in the streams. He came upon other villages and spoke of the plight of his own, but none had weavers to spare. Aponitalau's resolve to find a weaver for his village began to fade.

He felt the sun's steady heat on his back as he continued his journey. His legs felt heavy and his mouth, dry. He was very tired and was on the verge of giving up. This wasn't the adventure he thought it would be. As he despondently sat by a river to rest, a flash of colors caught his eye. He stood up and, to his amazement, saw about a hundred blankets that had been washed and laid out to dry. All those beautiful blankets! Each one was as lovely as the next. Quickly, he went in search of the weavers.

The women jumped in surprise as the overjoyed stranger came rushing to them. After he had calmed down, the young warrior told the women the story of his village, of how the villagers had stopped dreaming and had forgotten the old ways.

The women felt sorry for Aponitalau and his village. They brought him to their elders. Upon hearing his story, the elders met and decided to help Aponitalau's village by sending them one of their weavers. But which one?

The elders asked the women who among them would volunteer to help this faraway village. At first, all the women kept their eyes to the ground. None of them wanted to leave the village of their birth. Then, one young woman slowly lifted her eyes and in a soft voice said she would go. Everyone looked at her and nodded. Yes, she was the right one.

Imbangad was her name and, although young, she was a skilled weaver. She had lost her husband in a hunting accident and had no children. If she went with this warrior, she might find some happiness in the village on the far mountain. So she gathered her things, packed her loom, and said goodbye to her friends. After a few days, Aponitalau and Imbangad set out for his village.

The journey was long and tedious, but Aponitalau and Imbangad didn't mind because they were both distracted by their thoughts. Aponitalau felt like a hero. He only hoped that none of the other warriors had found a weaver. Imbangad, on the other hand, had mixed feelings. She was a little sad at having to leave her village, but she was also looking forward to a new life in her new home. She wasn't sure how the people of Aponitalau's village would receive her. She may be skillful, but was she as good as Bugan?

The villagers rejoiced at the arrival of Aponitalau and Imbangad. The other warriors had returned empty-handed, and the village had despaired. The elders immediately gifted Imbangad with Bugan's hut and loom. They showed her the vats where Bugan had dyed her threads and where she had laid them out to dry. They also pointed out the places where they thought Bugan had picked the fruits and roots with which to make the different colored dyes.

Aponitalau was given a hero's welcome. He was rewarded with a warrior's spear made of the hardest wood and the brightest steel. He was also given a handsome belt made of the shiniest *capiz* shells. The warrior's chest burst with pride.

The entire village turned out to celebrate. They roasted their fattest pig and brought out the *tapuey*, the sweet, fermented rice wine of which the people of the North are so fond. When their stomachs were full and their hearts a little lighter, they laid out their blankets and danced on them to celebrate the village's newfound life. The sound of merrymaking echoed throughout the night and into the wee hours of the morning.

Imbangad quickly settled into her new home. She loved Bugan's old hut and was proud of having been honored with Bugan's loom. She tilled the soil and planted new vegetables in the garden until it bloomed with string beans and cabbages, which Imbangad happily shared with her neighbors.

Imbangad found great comfort in her weaving. Into each blanket she put all her hopes and dreams. Everyday she sat under the eaves, looked out to the emerald mountains that Bugan loved, and wove her magic. She moved her body to the rhythm of the threads, throwing the baliga and pushing the gur-on, the sounds of weaving filling the village once again.

Imbangad wove blankets filled with the flowers, butterflies, and stars that the women so loved. She gifted the warriors and elders with blankets studded with deer, horses, snakes, and frogs to inspire them with strength and wisdom.

Imbangad had much for which to thank her new village.

In gratitude, she taught the other village women how to weave. They learned to value and love the craft, especially after they had nearly lost their dreams and with it, their old ways. In time the village prospered, and the weaving never stopped.

The wonderful Itneg dreams continue and their traditions with them, for, to this day, the Itneg women weave blankets as beautiful as those of their ancestors.

CHUN

by Marivi Soliven Blanco
Illustration by Arnel Mirasol

*P*itoy was the tallest of the neighborhood kids. And I was the broadest. As for Chun, Chun was...different. He was a thin, frail child with skin so pale it looked as though he never played outside. And to top that, Chun had little, slanted, creaseless eyes. Chun was Chinese.

Pitoy and I and the rest of our friends were Filipino, and we never let Chun forget the difference. We teased him about how his old uncles drooled at the mouth and how his mother set food at an altar honoring some long-dead ancestor.

We joked about his incense-scented home and the chopsticks he ate with and his father's skimpy *kamiseta*-and-*karsonsillo* outfits. In fact, if his father had not owned the corner candy store, we'd never have bothered to let Chun play with us. But there he was—surrounded by large, thick glass jars of chocolates and candies and salted nuts. Such a friend was useful to have around, in case any of us got hungry on an empty pocket.

We'd gather at the corner store and point out our favorite sweets with fat, greasy fingers. We'd gulp down the candies, scarcely managing to remove their crinkly wrappers. Then we'd scamper off, pretending to have forgotten to pay. But Chun always managed to make us pay up, through constant nagging or an insistent tugging at our sleeves. Perhaps we liked to torment him with the uncertainty of nonpayment. Perhaps that is why we begrudged him our coins after an afternoon of begging. But we never considered Chun one of us. Chun was simply...different.

As children's gangs go, there were certain rituals that we all followed to ensure membership in the inner circle. We'd blindfold the prospective member and give him either a plate of cold spaghetti or a plate of dead worms to eat. We almost never managed to gather enough worms to fill a plate, but then we could never decide which was worse: eating cold spaghetti, believing it was dead worms; or eating dead worms, believing it was cold spaghetti.

All of us—except, of course, that Mama's boy, Bastian, who chickened out on a plate of dead worms—had passed the test. All, that is, except Chun. At first he denied wanting to belong. But eventually, the urge to be one of us became so strong that he constantly nagged and tugged at our sleeves, begging to be put to the test. By then we had tired of the spaghetti-and-worms routine. We racked our brains for other tortuous feats.

One hot afternoon, while we were sitting by the curb rolling pebbles into the gutter, Pitoy had a flash of inspiration. "We'll have him climb into the manhole at the corner of Nicanor and Blanco!" he exclaimed. I instantly seconded his

idea. But when we put it to Chun, he withdrew into silence, refusing to reply to our goads.

"My parents believe that the filth of our ancestors lies beneath the streets. Going into a manhole would disturb all that ancient refuse," he finally said.

"Coward, coward, drooling, slit-eyed coward!" we chanted mercilessly, sending Chun running back to his incense-scented home.

We did not see him for several weeks after that. But one day we saw him sitting by the curb. It was the day someone on the Waterworks Commission decided to remove the manhole covers to dredge up the filth. We had somehow managed to loosen the lock of a fire hydrant on the curb, and were jumping around in a cool spray of high-pressure water. Pitoy's dog, Kulas, was just as lively, for it had been a hot summer and the water relieved the scorching heat on his thick, black coat. We'd run to the hydrant and let the gushing water push us back onto the street while we squealed with delight. Then it happened.

On one jubilant dash, Pitoy and Kulas collided, sending Pitoy staggering back and propelling Kulas straight into the manhole. We gasped—but none of us ventured to do more than peer into the black, forbidding hole. None of us knew what to do about Kulas's frantic whines. None of us even considered climbing into that hole to save Pitoy's dog. None, that is, except Chun. As I said, Chun was...different.

Having lingered on the outskirts all this time, he now stepped forward, dragging an old ladder that some telephone linesmen had neglected to stow away. Without a word, he pushed its end into the manhole, then clambered down. For what seemed an eternity we listened to him coax the frightened dog into his arms. Twice he called to us for help, but no one dared extend a hand, afraid of being pulled into that black, smelly hole.

We never figured out how he did it, but he finally emerged, full of scratches and bruises and filthy as sin, carrying Kulas in his arms. Grimly he handed the dog over to Pitoy. "I don't want to belong anymore. I am different and I always will be!" he declared, turning his back on us.

Perhaps we were ashamed to have been such cowards. And we hated him for that. We slowly drifted apart that summer—more so after our mothers got wind of what had happened, and decided to keep us apart.

When the rains came in June, and we were scowling over pages and pages of clean, new notebooks, we heard that Chun had moved away. His family had found a better corner on which to set up their candy store. We never found out where that was, but we figured it was in a place called Chinatown—where everyone else was...different.

I have not met Chun since. I am older now and many of my young nieces and nephews have slit-eyed friends with pale, unsunned skin and frail bodies. But they cannot tell the difference.

I often wish I also had never seen a difference—for, in fact, there was none—when I was once their age.

THE DAUGHTER OF THE WIND

by Angelo Rodriguez Lacuesta

Illustration by Auri Asuncion Yambao

For many weeks now, Luisa couldn't sleep well. All throughout summer she was sad and restless, flitting from corner to corner, wandering aimlessly among the clouds and sunbeams. During the long nights she fretted and sighed to herself, moving silently over the ocean waves, gazing mournfully at the mirror surface of the sea.

At night the water was cold and dark, and though she heard her 77 sisters calling for her with low whistles and traveling whispers, Luisa ignored them purposely. She glided and rolled and tumbled over the waters, and swept and spun and swooped down on the crests of the waves.

"Luisa!" her sisters whispered sharply. Their airy voices cut through the night with the sharpness of rain, stinging her ears with their coldness. "You must rest and gather your strength, for the day you will need it is fast approaching!"

At this reminder Luisa sobbed quietly and without tears, for although she dreaded that day, she couldn't show her fear to her father or, for that matter, to her 77 sisters.

Her father was known for his senseless fits of rage. Whenever Luisa angered him with her playfulness, he'd speak with deafening claps of thunder and vicious bolts of lightning that terrified her. And her sisters had taken after their father — quick-tempered, loud, and often unpredictable. When they were angry, they let loose a chorus of shrieks and howls so fearsome that Luisa would shudder and flee into the clouds.

Luisa was the youngest daughter of The Wind. And one day she would become like her sisters: a vengeful, terrible Typhoon. It was her destiny. Since she was small she had often felt traces of the power within her so that she often surprised herself with her own strength. Whenever she played on the sandy shores she'd sometimes rub her back against the tall trunks of trees, and their leaves would shudder and shake violently. When she laughed as she often did as a child, the sound disturbed the tall grass on the islands and blew dead leaves across the summer fields. Dogs howled and barked, and even grown men grew nervous at the sound of her giggles. And when she swam in the sea, she marvelled at the deep, dizzying whirlpools she dug in the waters.

But being a real Typhoon was quite different. She had seen many of her sisters reach their fateful day, when they had finally grown and gathered enough strength to blow across the waters and the islands, to fly wild and angry along the shores and river banks.

Among the strongest and oldest of her sisters was Ate Yoling. She was one of her father's favorites. He had nurtured and guided her carefully so that when Ate Yoling's time came she had grown so fierce that even her sisters feared her. On her day of reckoning she spiralled into the sea so swiftly that the sky shook with thunder and lightning. She careened across the waters so recklessly that fishing boats were swallowed in the tide. And when she came to the islands, she swept the waters so powerfully that gigantic waves leapt into the air and swallowed the seaside villages. With her rough, windy hands she tore down trees and huts, wrenching roofs away and tossing them into rainswept streets. She smashed houses and cars, shook buildings, and twisted bridges.

But what distubed Luisa the most were the men and women who were swept away, the fishermen who were drowned, and the families who became as wrecked and scattered as their match-stick houses. Although that was a long time ago, she remembered it clearly.

And now it was nearly her turn to be a full-fledged Typhoon. Even her powerful Ate Yoling could sense her misgivings. "I can feel your fear, littlest sister. Don't be so weak when you need to be collecting your strength."

"But," Luisa said, "perhaps I don't want to be strong at all..."

"But you must be!" Ate Yoling shot back, her icy words freezing in the air. "You are a Typhoon! That is your destiny!" The clouds began to grow as thin and dark as Ate Yoling's hair.

"Look at the islands below," Yoling commanded, and Luisa could not disobey her.

She peered through the rain clouds at a large island with a wide bay cut into it like a mouth. The bay was filled with ships of all sizes, carrying huge crates and metal boxes that glinted like silver in the morning sun. Luisa could see men working on the boats and on the docks. But the water down there had turned dull and dark, even in bright sunlight. Its foul smell reached even their windy palace high among the clouds.

From the bay a threadlike river ran into the land. The water turned muddy-brown with dirt and refuse as it twisted past houses and buildings. Where it ran beside huge factories that hummed with machinery, the river lay still as a swamp, its surface black and sticky with a strange, shiny, foul-smelling liquid. The factories pumped up steady streams of grimy smoke that smelled of poison. *The stench down there must be even greater,* Luisa thought, and she wondered how people could stand it.

"That is what people do to the wind and water," Ate Yoling whispered. "And what they do to the wind and water, they do to us. For we ourselves are wind and water."

Luisa could only accept this with sorrow.

When the fateful day came at last, Luisa felt strong and ready. Early in the morning her father, The Wind, called her with a silver streak of lightning to his great, cloudy courtyard. Luisa emerged from a huge white cloud and stood tall and strong before her father and all her 77 sisters.

She had dressed in all her finery. She wore a dress of woven vapor, so sheer that the clouds passed right through it freely. A belt of thin grey mist wound around her waist. On her head and shoulders was a veil of the lightest rain clouds, so that a thin sheet of rain lightly covered her beautiful face. On her fingers and ear lobes she wore gems of ice cut like flawless diamonds. Trapped inside the jewels were tiny bolts of white lightning that sparkled in the darkening sky.

Luisa raised her arms, and around her the clouds and the sky heaved and boiled. It grew darker and darker until only she and her sisters were the only sources of brightness. But Luisa easily outshone the others. Her sisters almost couldn't bear to look at her beauty and light and strength.

After a long silence, her stunned father spoke. "Well done, my daughter," he said.

But Luisa drowned out his words with the roaring wind of her wake, as she curled her body and, with a graceful arc, dove straight to the islands and the sea below.

So many islands dotted the sea that Luisa couldn't even begin to count them. There were perhaps thousands or even tens of thousands of them, shining like multi-colored stars.

In her childhood long, long ago Luisa had visited many beautiful islands, but she had never thought there were so many more, each more beautiful than the last. As she roamed, she saw islands of all shapes and sizes. There were islands that reached the horizon and there were some that seemed too small even for a man to stand on. There were islands fringed with rocks, with pink and gray and white sand, with long green grass, and with the coconut trees of her childhood. She saw islands that grew thick forests, and these hummed with the sounds of birds and insects. She saw others that had nothing but dry sand and rock.

But there were many islands that were surrounded by big fishing boats and covered with the roofs of houses. Indeed, some of these were the once-lonely places she had visited before. Men had put up tall buildings and winding roads, and some had even put up factories. Wherever there were men, Luisa noticed that the wind and water around their islands had turned dark and dirty.

Angered by her discovery, Luisa headed for the large island that Yoling had pointed out to her many weeks before. She didn't release her wind and rain yet, but kept her immense power inside, where it surged and hummed through her veins. The island's dirty, curving mouth grew ever larger as she flew silently and swiftly towards it.

Across the bay, men had built tall buildings of steel and glass that looked across the sea and shone in the sun like towers of flames. Nearby, huge factories made curious, rumbling, breathing sounds like huge, dumb animals, snorting out thick spirals of the black smoke she could smell from above. Scattered all around were little houses, their roofs like pebbles on beaches, bright with all the colors of the rainbow. Past the houses and the buildings were slow-moving chains of cars, breathing out the same black smoke that came from the factories, stuck end-to-end on the tangled strands of roads and highways. Winding through the island like a long black eel was the river whose waters stood almost still.

Luisa knew that she could make the buildings creak and shiver with her passing. With a flick of her fingers she could shatter their glass walls. With the merest gesture she could plow through the houses, blowing them apart with strong winds and drowning them in thick sheets of rain. With a vengeful laugh she could send the cars flying end over end across the roads. She could make the river rise above its banks with a simple snapping of the shawl so that the many factories would drown in their own black muck.

She could do what many of her sisters had done. And because she knew that she was more powerful than any of

them—even Ate Yoling—Luisa knew she could do more. She remembered Ate Yoling's words. Luisa herself was made of wind and water. It was her destiny to be a Typhoon. She felt the power rise and boil within her, like the waves of the ocean. How it yearned to burst forth with the rush of fierce winds and the explosion of rain!

But as she passed men in their container ships and fishing boats she saw them look at the sky in terror as her winds blew across their salt-stained faces. As she glided along the shore the saw little boys with sun-browned skin fleeing from the growing waves. And as she snaked along river banks she saw women in wooden houses weep and shiver, hoping that she wouldn't come. Poor people who slept on the streets and sidewalks stirred and opened their eyes as she passed, and although Luisa had not summoned her wind-strength yet, the city folk felt her presence in the air, the strange, icy shadow of her passing.

Luisa felt the fear around her. She felt people cringe from the merest touch of her winds, as easily as the trees swayed and the bridges trembled. And so she felt her old feelings return. Try hard as she could, she couldn't feel anger for those who dwelled on the islands below. Those who had built tall majestic buildings and beautiful houses and bridges, but destroyed the wind and water around them. Those who walked the streets proudly and happily and bravely, but didn't know they were at the mercy of the water and the wind. For them Luisa could only feel a strange pity and sadness.

She felt her power crumble into a sadness so great that instead of rough winds and heavy rains, she let loose a soft shower of tears, scattered all over the islands by a cool, gentle breeze.

And so a light rain fell softly on people's heads and sprinkled the fields and sidewalks. It fell upon cars, bridges, buildings, and factories. Luisa whispered into people's ears and blew through littered streets, gardens, and houses. It rained and blew for days, the rain and wind softly enveloping the islands with the coldness and sadness of Luisa's tears and sighs. What would have been the most terrifying Typhoon in history never came.

Luisa knew it was time to return when she saw two faint bursts of lightning in the eastern corner of the sky. Although she had seen her father's signal many times before, calling for her other sisters, never had she been more afraid than now. After all, she had disobeyed him and shamed herself in front of her sisters. She had turned her back on her destiny.

But when she arrived at the palace of The Wind, beautiful and resplendent even in her sorrow, she saw that her father didn't seem at all disappointed. For The Wind knew and understood all along that Luisa's destiny was different.

She was to be a gentle, caressing wind, a quiet, tender rain. The softness of her whispers and tears would serve to remind people of everything they had done to the wind and water. And the coldness of her wind and rain would remind them of their utter weakness before the daughters of The Wind.

Luisa's rain fell and her winds blew, soft and cold, for a very, very long time. For although she didn't become a Typhoon, she knew she was still the most powerful daughter of The Wind.

THE MAN
WHO HATED BIRDS

by Leoncio P. Deriada

Illustration by Felix Mago Miguel

There was a man who hated birds. He hated every single one of them—little birds, big birds, white birds, brown birds, black birds.

When the birds sang, it was noise to his ears. He threw stones at them and shook the branches of the trees where they perched and built their nests. The man thought of a way to get rid of them.

Without his knowing it, the birds were thinking, too. They didn't like the man who threw stones at them and drove them away from the trees. "Let's eat his *palay* to teach him a lesson," said the birds to one another.

The man's hatred for the birds grew when he saw them eating his palay. He drove them away, but the birds returned after a few minutes and continued eating.

"Go away, you awful creatures!" shouted the man and threw even more stones at the birds.

The birds left the palay, but didn't fly very far away.

They alighted on the branches of a big mango tree in the middle of the field. The man knew that, after a few minutes, they would return to eat his palay.

The man had an idea. At last he would get rid of all these birds! The man smiled wickedly.

He went to the woods nearby and gathered the sap of the *tipolo* tree.

The tipolo was a big tree that looked like the giant jackfruit tree. Its sap was white and thick and was a powerful glue.

The man climbed the mango tree in the middle of his field and carefully applied the tipolo sap on each of its branches. Soon the mango tree was covered with this unexpected trap.

Then the man drove the birds away from his palay. In one movement, the birds flew away. But they didn't go far. They flew in circles above the field. They were so many— big birds, little birds, white birds, brown birds, black birds— that they seemed to be a giant cloud above the mango tree and the field.

Then together, they swooped down and alighted on the branches of the mango tree. Suddenly, there was a lot of noise. The man knew that his trap had worked. The pained birdcalls were music to his ears.

"Tonight I will have a great feast," said the man to himself, thinking of roasted and fried birds. He licked his lips in anticipation.

The man took a big sack and climbed up the tree. He meant to catch each bird, remove its feathers, and put it in

his sack. He'd kill them later at home. Whistling in joy, the man reached out for the first bird. But in one movement, all the birds spread their wings and flew.

Instantly the mango tree was uprooted and lifted in the air! And with it, the wicked man.

Terribly afraid, the man held on tightly to a branch. Soon he saw that he was floating high above the barrio.

"Help! Help!" shouted the man, but no one heard him. He was too high up.

"Tweet! Tweet!" answered the little *maya*s.

The crows cawed.

The pigeons squawked.

The parrots screeched.

"Chirp! Chirp!" cried all the other birds.

Soon the man saw the sea under him. Then a little rocky island.

The birds flew downward until the uprooted mango tree was standing steadily on the little island.

The man jumped off the tree and found himself alone. There was no one in sight.

"Help! Help!" called the man desperately.

The birds screeched and squawked at him. The sun shone brighter and hotter, and the tipolo sap that glued the birds' feet to the branches of the mango tree began to melt.

The man was very angry. He had nowhere to go. And he didn't know how to swim. He picked up some stones and threw them at the birds. The birds screeched and squawked and together, spread their wings and flew away, leaving the mango tree and the wicked man alone on the island.

The birds returned to the man's field and had a great feast. They ate all his palay.

As for the man who hated birds, he was trapped on the island. Nobody came to save him. In fact, Grandfather says, he is there still.

THE BLANKET

by Maria Elena Paterno
Illustration by Joanne de León

It is May, and the Cordillera mountains stand impassive and mute, green-gray and misty, as they have been since they were thrust up from the ocean one hundred fifty million years ago.

There are two women named Gaia, mother and daughter. They look alike, but are different, because they are of two generations.

The daughter speaks: "My name is Gaia, and I am fifteen years old. I have lived in this village all my life, but now I am going away.

"I am going away to study in the city, where few people know me, where there will be many new things to see and hear and taste. It will be exciting. I am almost packed, save for this blanket my mother is weaving for me. Everyday I check to see if it is finished because she says as soon as it is done, I may go.

"She sits here in the morning when the sunlight is soft.

And then again in the afternoon, till early evening. Sometimes she tells me to bring a lamp, so she can weave at night. Everyday, it is the same. She does not speak when she weaves, only the sound of the wood clacking in a rhythm and my mother's body bending slowly to arrange the threads.

"Wood, thread, and flesh—you would have thought they were one.

"She is strapped to her loom. 'Why do you need to be strapped,' I ask her, 'like a prisoner?'

"But she only smiles. 'When you weave, you will understand,' she says.

"But I will never weave. I am going away to study. I will become a doctor. When will she finish this blanket?"

Then the mother speaks: "I am a weaver, and my name is Gaia. It is a name strange to us, and does not come easily to our lips. An old name of an ancient people, it means 'Earth.'

"My daughter is named Gaia, too. But she is different. She wants to go away. She sits impatiently, watching me weave, waiting for me to finish this blanket. Her grandmother says that I must let her go, but there are so many things I want to tell her still. Only I do not know how."

The grandmother is 61 and blind, but her back is straight as she sits in the sun. She sits with a blanket around her, for the mountain air blows chill. She sits, and, unseeing, she listens. And feels.

In this cold dawn, as fifteen-year-old Gaia waits at her mother's loom, impatient to be off, as weaver Gaia builds a design, thread by thread, old Luning sits in the sun and feels the child's urgency, the mother's resoluteness.

32

She had gone away when she was her granddaughter's age, sure she would never be back. Wanting to escape the mountain's shadow, she worked very hard in the missionary school, learned English, and went to the city with an American family. She became a doctor. Later she married a young man with bright eyes, a doctor like her, also from the mountains.

When she became pregnant, he wanted to go back home.

"But what is there to go back to?" she had argued. "They do not believe in our science. They will not accept our medicine. They will not understand!"

"We can help." He was calm and determined. "We can make them understand. Our child belongs in those mountains."

The old woman smiles, remembering her anguish. Like her granddaughter now. "Gaia," she calls, "come sit by us. I want to tell you something before you go."

Thinking that this is a good sign, that perhaps she will go soon, the girl obeys.

"If you go to the city, you may never see us weave again," the old voice says gently. The girl looks at her grandmother in surprise. She had not thought of that.

"Watch. See how straight the threads are, how taut. They have to be, for the weave to be even and tight and the blanket, warm. This is the warp"—here, motioning with her strong, wrinkled, brown hands—"and this is the weft. Watch how the threads mesh."

Gaia sits quietly, settled in her mother's rhythm, the rhythm of body and loom, wood, thread, and flesh, one.

Her grandmother continues. "Here are the sticks to set

the design. Here, the shuttle to bring the thread across. It is simple, yet not simple. Watch."

The child watches. Her body moves slightly, without her knowing it, to her mother's rhythm. She would stop if she knew, but she doesn't.

She watches the designs emerging, like secrets of the thread. They are familiar to her—the star with eight points, the eye—she has seen them many times before. But this is new, this pattern of the star in the eye, diamond motifs repeating. She watches the designs integrating, warp and weft meshing. She watches the weaving, and wonders why she has never seen the magic before.

"How do you know what the design will look like?" she asks shyly, interested in spite of herself. "How do you think of the pattern?"

Gaia, the weaver, looks at her daughter and smiles. "You see it in your mind's eye," she answers.

Gaia the would-be doctor gives an impatient snort. Her mother always speaks in riddles. What is a mind's eye?

Her grandmother intervenes. "The weaver plans the design," she says. "The weaver must know how much thread to use and what colors these must be. Then the threads are set on the loom. You have watched us do that, so you know how long that takes. Only then can the weaving begin. The weaver must know her threads, her loom. It is skill, but it is also love. To lose oneself in the rhythm of the wood; to build the pattern, the designs; to make a blanket to keep you warm. This, you see, is our gift—the rhythm of the loom, the colors and pattern, the warmth. Your blanket is almost finished. Soon you may go."

Gaia does not see her mother's face bent over the loom. There is pain there, of having to let go of her firstborn, but there is also peace, the peace that she would like to give to her daughter. It is the peace of living in one place and wanting to die there. Gaia does not see her mother's face because she is wrestling with her own feelings. She wants to go and yet, now, she does not want to go.

She touches the blanket. "I do not want it to be finished," she says softly. "Not yet."

Her grandmother smiles, and her black eyes seem moist. "Let me tell you a story.

"When your grandfather took me back here," she says, "I was angry. I did not want to be here, this primitive little village, these mountains, these people who did not believe as we did. And so far from the city!

"But he insisted that our child grow up in the mountains. What could I do? I loved him, and so I followed. But I was not happy to be back.

"We arrived at night because the bus had broken down and the roads were bad. We slept under blankets because it was cold.

"But that morning, the child in me kicked and I woke up. It was still dark. There were a few stars left in the sky. I wrapped a blanket around me and went out.

"I sat for a while under those stars in silence. The child had stopped moving, and it seemed that the whole world had stopped, it was so still and quiet. My fingers felt as if they were going to freeze right off my hand, but I did not want to go back in.

"Soon it came—the light, the strange, gray light that

makes shapes in the mist.

"And then a different light, a white light. You have seen it, Gaia, the light that comes at dawn, the fresh white light that comes from everywhere, mountain light.

"Then the mists lifted. It became warm and the dawn light was gone.

"But I will never forget that morning. It was such a new morning.

"I went back in the house. Your grandfather was awake. He was making a fire for the coffee. The small flames were just beginning to catch, and he was blowing mightily on the coals. There was an orange glow on his face that lit his eyes. And I laughed, because I was happy.

"As soon as we were settled and had made our home, I began to weave. It is not easy to be a weaver. It took me many weeks to learn. But I learned.

"I wove a strap with which to carry my baby. I put many colors in it, and I edged it with stars. 'Why must you put stars,' they said, 'it is only a sling for the child.' But those stars on the strap were my dawn stars, and they would carry my child. I did not tell them. They would have thought I was mad.

"Later, when my baby was born, I carried her everywhere with me—on my rounds at the hospital and up mountainsides to visit sick people who did not believe in hospitals. The strap held her close to me as that dawn had cradled me many months before."

But here the girl interrupts, "That baby—" She looks at her mother, then at her grandmother, and tries to imagine them as they were many, many years ago. Her grandmother, eyes bright and seeing, climbing a mountain with her daughter. Her mother, a baby in a strap at her side. "That baby was—"

Her mother leans over and takes her hand. "We know you have to go away," she says. "We know how much you want to go."

Gaia looks at her mother. *We have the same eyes,* she thinks suddenly. Aloud she says, "I will come back. I must go away now, but I will come back. I promise."

To herself she makes another promise: *I will learn to weave.*

THE GEM

by Lina B. Diaz de Rivera
Illustration by Albert Gamos

Santa Ana is a quiet, little district in the south of Manila. In the mid-nineteenth century, it was a favorite retreat of very important people. They built big beautiful summer houses with lovely lawns that faced, not the street, but the rippling Pasig River. When they held receptions in the dry months of the year, their guests took boat rides to small piers that led to white *galerias*.

As in most Philippine towns in those days, the center of the community was the church. The Santa Ana Church was lovely and imposing. It sat on a hill that overlooked the river.

Paro lived in Santa Ana. She was eight years old. She had dark, wavy hair that her mother plaited for her. When worn loose, it reached the rosy heels of her small *cochos*.

Her mother *Aling* Otay teased her that someday many young men would try to catch a glimpse of her tiny feet peeping from beneath the hem of her hoisted *cola*. Her father

Maestro Ninoy agreed. Paro loved her mother dearly, but she adored her father, and she flashed her small dimples whenever he called her "My gem."

Paro's father, Catalino Nazario, was a teacher at Escuela Catolica. He and his wife, Rosa Rivera, and their children, Paro and Paco, were ordinary people, but they owned a piece of land on a choice part of the riverside—at the point where the land jutted toward the east. Many expatriates offered to buy their property, but the Nazarios wouldn't sell their treasure for anything. They were told that they could buy a better piece of land if they sold what they had, but the family wanted to remain close to the river. They knew that the river nurtured the soil.

Maestro Ninoy's grandfather was gifted this piece of land by an old parish priest in whose faithful service Lelong Popoy spent the best years of his life. As a young man Popoy worked as a sacristan, then as a clerk at the *convento*. He was one of the few literate Filipinos of his time. The Franciscan *cura paroco* defied tradition by appointing, not a Spanish seminarian, but Popoy as his personal secretary.

The cura had hoped to convince him to be a priest, but Popoy chose to marry a young lady who came to church morning and afternoon. Before the cura died, he awarded Popoy the title to the property beside the river. In those days most of the estates around the church and the *calle real* were owned by the Archbishop of Manila and by the religious orders.

Lelong Popoy's ability to read and write had been handed down from generation to generation to the sons of the Nazario family. But in Paro's generation Maestro Ninoy insisted that his daughter learn her letters as thoroughly as his son, Paco. By the time Paro and Paco were old enough to go to school, there had been a royal decree giving the people of *las islas Filipinas* the right to an education. Paro and Paco went to Escuela Catolica, where Maestro Ninoy taught reading, writing, arithmetic, history, music, sewing, carpentry, as well as catechism and good manners.

Paro loved to read fables, stories from the Bible, and tales about the lives of the saints. Next to reading Paro enjoyed swimming. She learned to swim at almost the same time she learned to walk and talk. On warm days Paro spent as much time as she could in the river she loved or on its banks. With the laughing river merrily flowing behind her, Paro sat on her favorite boulder from where she could look up at the church on the hill.

She knew the story of the Blessed Virgin by heart, as she was venerated by the people under the title Nuestra Señora de los Desamparados. Her parents told her that the title meant "Our Lady of the Forsaken." Paro's mother chose to name her after the *patrona*. Her full name, Maria Amparo, was derived from the Virgin's title. Her brother's full name, Francisco, honored the gentle saint, Francis of Assisi, and the priests who had been friends of the family for generations. Aling Otay cherished her devotion to her favorite Franciscan saints and often took Paro to church for her devotionals.

One of the happiest days of Paro's life was when she received her first Holy Communion on the Christmas Day after her seventh birthday. Before walking to church for the ceremony, Paro's mother showed her an old *camagong* box. Aling Otay kept the black box in the farthest corner of her big *aparador*. It was full of earrings, bracelets, and rings placed in tiny, special compartments, as well as necklaces, *painetas*, and jewelled *agojillas* that Paro's mother wore on special occasions.

That day her mother picked out a small golden ring with a beautiful green stone. "It's time you wore this gem," Aling Otay whispered to Paro.

"Oh, Nanay. It's beautiful," cried Paro. "Are you really giving it to me?"

"Yes, *hija*. It's an emerald. It belonged to your great-great-grandmother Rivera. Each daughter of the family received a gem on her first Holy Communion. There is a ruby, a pearl, a sapphire, and a topaz in our collection. Since you were born in May, I am giving you the emerald, your birthstone. You are to wear the ring until it gets too small for your finger. By then a Rivera maiden is usually getting ready for her wedding. Should she decide to enter the convent, she gets a plain band for her religious profession."

"How lovely, Nanay. But the ring seems a little too big for me."

"It's all right. We'll slip a piece of cloth to keep it in place. Soon you won't need the padding."

From that day on, Paro wore the ring, removing it only when she went for a swim.

One summer day she went for a dip as usual, leaving her clothes on her favorite boulder. When she returned to retrieve her things, she didn't find her ring in the small side pocket of her *saya*, where she remembered keeping it. She scoured the grass beside the boulder, thinking that the ring might have slipped out of her pocket. It wasn't there.

Her mother was upset and advised Paro to give the riverside another round of searching. She also reminded her to whisper a prayer to San Antonio, another Franciscan, the patron saint of lost things.

Paro frantically searched around the boulder and the pathways that she took that afternoon. She reminded herself that the gem was as green as the grass beneath her feet. So she had to look very carefully.

Not finding the ring, she slid on the grass, placed her arms on the boulder, and sobbed. She prayed as she wept quietly and, from time to time, looked up at the church on the hill, as if summoning the aid of all the venerated saints.

As she wept she sensed a presence. She straightened up and met a pair of the greenest eyes she had ever seen. They belonged to a young priest garbed in the familiar coarse, brown Franciscan cassock. She had a feeling that, though she had never met him before, he seemed familiar.

"I'm sorry I startled you, Paro," the priest said in a deep, resonant voice. It had the sound of all the kindness in the world. It was a compelling voice, one that would be very effective before a crowd.

"It's all right, Father," Paro said, holding out her hand to grasp his. She brought his hand to her forehead as a sign of respect.

"I am Father Antonio, a friend of your mother's. I paid her a visit. She was talking to me when she realized that it was almost Angelus time and you hadn't returned. I volunteered to remind you to go home before the sun disappears completely." As the priest spoke, the setting sun framed the church steeple, and Paro was momentarily blinded by the light, as well as by something that she couldn't quite identify. It seemed to radiate above the priest's head.

"I'm so sorry you had to bother, Father," said Paro. "I was looking for something that's very precious to me. But...but I haven't found it." Her eyes watered with tears.

As she sobbed into her palms, she felt the priest's hand on her shoulder. He spoke again. "Yes, your mother told me. And no, you haven't lost it. I'm sure you've only misplaced it. You'll find it again. You see, you and your family know how to cherish your most precious possessions. This land, for example, and the river. And, of course, your faith. Then he turned towards the church. "See your church on the hill, Paro?"

"Yes, Father. I love our church. It's very beautiful. Even more beautiful than the big churches in Intramuros, for it sits on a hill. It's the only church in Manila that sits on a hill."

"You're right, Paro. It looks like a gem sitting on a mound of granite. It's very much like your faith and the faith of your family, which you have cherished for hundreds of years. Your trust in the Lord will never be lost. You may lose material things like your house, your ring, or even your river, but your faith will always abide in you. You have been given God's grace."

"Oh, Father Antonio, I hope you're right," Paro sobbed, although she couldn't quite understand all that he had said. "But help me pray to your namesake to find my ring for me just the same."

"I will, but now I must go. I need to cross the bridge before sundown to visit a friend in Hulo. Goodbye now. Go

and catch the Angelus with your family." He waved farewell.

In the falling darkness, Paro was left puzzled, a little afraid, but somewhat happy. The beautiful sound of church bells suddenly filled the air, jolting Paro from her thoughts. She ran to the house and saw her mother waiting for her at the galeria, waving something in her hand.

"Hija, your ring has been here all along," Aling Otay said.

"Where, Nanay?"

"You put it under your clothes in your aparador. I took a chance that you'd kept it there. Calling on San Antonio, I felt beneath the folded linen, and there it was! Here, put it on."

"Oh, Nanay. Father Antonio was right."

"Father who? Oh, you mean San Antonio."

"No, Nanay. I mean Father..." Suddenly, Paro's eyes widened in realization. "Oh yes, San Antonio, of course. Nanay, do you know the color of San Antonio's eyes?"

"What are you talking about, hija? Let's go in and pray the Angelus. Your father and Paco are waiting for us."

"Oh, Nanay. But I do know the color of San Antonio's eyes. They're green!"

Aling Otay couldn't understand her daughter's whimsical nature sometimes. Maestro Ninoy always did. She smiled at her approaching husband and son.

As Paro responded to every *Dios Te Salve Maria,* she gazed at her family, her ring, the river, then at the church on the hill. The setting sun covered them all in a golden light.

LITTLE BIRD, LITTLE FISH, AND THE TWO ELEPHANTS

by Ino M. Manalo

Illustration by Robert A. Alejandro

In an age of traders and travelers, an age long passed, a ship was sailing on the wild, dark sea. In a tiny bed at the far end of the ship a little boy lay awake all night crying.

The boy was crying because he remembered a faraway land with green mountains and blue rivers. He remembered watching river barges sail by with their cargo of jade and rice. And how his toy boats bobbed up and down with the waves.

He was crying because he remembered the softness of his mother's voice and the way she held him close to her heart when it was very dark. Most of all, he remembered her teaching him to sing.

"Little Bird, Little Bird," she would say, "sing a new song."

And he would sing. His song floated above the tiled roofs, and the neighbors who heard it would say, "He sings like a little bird."

But Little Bird's family was very poor. They had barely enough to eat. One day the food ran out. But Little Bird's parents had sold everything of any value. They had nothing left—except their children. To keep the rest of the family from starving, Little Bird's parents made the painful decision to sell him.

In those days little children could be bought and sold. Merchants bought them to make them into servants.

All his parents could do was make sure Little Bird went to a kind-hearted merchant. His mother couldn't stop weeping. As he was taken away, she whispered between sobs, "Sing, Little Bird, don't forget to sing."

But Little Bird didn't sing for a very long time. He only cried.

The merchant brought him on a journey to a great city in the Land of Temples. Here Little Bird was turned over to his new master. Diego Belloso was a big man with a large nose and a thick beard. Unlike Little Bird, his skin was white.

Little Bird knew all about him. He had been told many stories about his new master by the cook. Diego Belloso's home was very far away. He had traveled all around the world before coming to the Land of Temples. There he had befriended the king, who often sent him on voyages.

One day Diego Belloso took Little Bird on a long voyage on a ship with many red sails. The red sails reminded him of his toy boats. In the evenings the sound of the wind gently blowing into the sails reminded him of his mother's soft voice in the darkness. It was at these times Little Bird cried.

On one such night Diego Belloso approached him and

said, "So what the cook said is true, little one. You spend your nights in tears. Tell me, poor Bird, why are you crying?"

Little Bird choked back his tears, but didn't answer.

Diego Belloso spoke again, but more softly, "Cook told me how you were taken from your home. I know your land, for I have been there many times. It is a land of green mountains and blue rivers filled with barges carrying rice and jade." As Diego Belloso spoke Little Bird's tears welled up once again. "I'm sorry, little one. I seem to be making things worse," the kind man said. "Would you like to go out on the deck where it is cooler?"

Little Bird got up to follow the white man. Outside they stood looking at the waves for a few moments before Diego Belloso spoke again. "I, too, came from a faraway land. And I also left my family behind. But this is the way it must be when you travel on the sea. You must learn to find new friends and families."

"You mean I can have a new family?" Little Bird asked hopefully.

"Oh yes, whoever you choose or whoever chooses you becomes your family."

The next morning Diego Belloso asked Little Bird to work in the hold. It was very dark below deck. He could barely see at first. Then he noticed two strange shapes. His eyes widened and his jaw dropped. There were two elephants in the hold!

Little Bird had seen elephants before, in the forests of the Land of the Temples. But surely these two in the hold were ghosts!

The boy ran to his master as fast as he could and quickly

told him about the two ghosts. Diego Belloso laughed and said, "The elephants are gifts from the King of the Land of Temples. I am delivering them to the governor of the country of many islands called Filipinas."

Little Bird was quite ashamed. But Diego Belloso spoke again. "When we get to Filipinas, I will take you to my sister who lives there. She owns a big house. There are monkeys on her beds and parrots on her window sills. She is sure to like you, Little Bird."

From that day on Little Bird was in charge of the two elephants. He fed and washed them everyday. He liked to tickle their trunks. And whenever they were restless and sad, he sang to them. He sang of green mountains and blue rivers, of toy boats and soft voices. As he sang, the elephants quieted down. Perhaps, they understood Little Bird's song because they, too, were far from the land of their birth.

Days later the ship docked at a great port to buy more supplies for the trip. The great port was a place where the traders and travelers of the world met. Its harbor was filled with ships of all sizes and its market was filled with people of all sorts. As Little Bird explored the crowded alleys he came upon a fat old woman and a young girl, who smiled at him. Little Bird smiled back, then asked the little girl's name.

"My name is Little Fish," said the girl.

At this, Little Bird laughed.

The girl became very angry. "Why are you laughing? My name's not funny! My people have many boats, and our houses are built on stilts over the water. I learned to swim before I could walk, and I was the best swimmer in our village. That is how I got my name," Little Fish said proudly.

Little Bird stopped laughing. "I'm sorry. I wasn't laughing at your name. I was laughing because my name is Little Fish. You see, we're both named after animals."

Little Fish giggled. But when Little Bird asked his new friend about her home, she didn't answer right away. After a long silence, she said, "I was taken from my home a year ago. Pirates came and killed my people and burned our houses. They took me with them and sold me to a merchant. The woman I am with is kind to me, but she is keeping an eye on me for the merchant."

Little Bird put his hand on his new friend's shoulder and said, "I was also sold and taken from my home."

Little Bird knew who Little Fish's master was. He often saw him on the pier. He was a very thin man with a very thin face. And he carried a long sharp sword at his side.

The children spent the next few days running through the market; sitting on the pier and waving to the sailors; and swimming in the sea. Sometimes they swam all the way to a little island in the middle of the harbor to see who was faster. Little Fish always won. Other times they fed the elephants together. When the elephants had been fed and the sun had gone down, Little Fish would ask Little Bird to sing. As Little Bird sang, the sailors on their decks pretended that his singing didn't make them cry.

Little Fish liked to say that the elephants understood every word of his song. Little Bird smiled when she said this. It made him happy to think of the animals as his friends.

Little Fish's master grew angry whenever he saw the two children together. He'd shake his long sword and scold the girl's guardian for letting her roam freely. The old woman always answered, "They're only children. Let them play. They won't think of escaping."

One afternoon Little Bird found Little Fish crying. When he asked her why, she sobbed, "I'm going to the Land of Sand."

"What will you do there?"

"I'll be the servant of a prince. He has many horses and many tents filled with all kinds of toys and treasures."

"But where will you swim?"

"I don't know," Little Fish wailed as her tears fell into the waves. "I can't swim in sand."

The next morning Little Bird awoke to a lot of noise. On the deck he met the cook, who told him they were leaving the great port that afternoon. They were sailing for the islands of Filipinas. Suddenly, from the pier below, Little Bird heard a familiar voice. The boy looked over the ship's railing. He saw two big men dragging Little Fish along the pier. The old woman walked behind them with a sad face. They were taking Little Fish to the Land of Sand!

The cook saw the child being dragged away. He warned Little Bird not to cause any trouble. If Little Bird helped his friend, Diego Belloso's ship might not be allowed to leave the harbor. Little Fish's master had many powerful friends.

At that moment Little Fish's master appeared. The poor girl pleaded with him, but the merchant remained silent. Then Little Bird saw his hand flash in the light. He had slapped Little Fish!

Little Bird dashed down to the pier. He threw himself at the merchant. "You cruel, cruel man!" he screamed. The merchant laughed in his face. Then he called for his men to

take hold of Little Bird.

As the men grabbed him, Little Bird saw Diego Belloso on the deck of their ship. He saw that the white man wanted to help him, but the other sailors were holding him back. Little Bird noticed the two elephants in the distance. They were swaying to and fro. He knew that meant they were very nervous.

"Help! Help!" Little Bird shouted. "Help! Help!" he called again. The elephants continued swaying. Just then, Little Bird had an idea. Breaking free from the men, he climbed up a pile of boxes. Standing alone above the crowd, Little Bird began to sing. He sang of green mountains and blue rivers. He sang of toy boats bobbing up and down with the waves. He sang of voices whispering in the darkness. As he sang, every ship in the harbor seemed to stop. Every person on the pier fell silent. Everyone was listening to Little Bird's song.

Suddenly shouts were heard. The elephants were angry! They strained against their chains. *CRACK!* They ran towards Little Bird. The merchant and his men fled. Down the long pier thundered the two elephants. They stopped in front of the pile of boxes where Little Bird stood. The boy quickly climbed down to hug the trunks of his two great friends.

Meanwhile, Little Fish had broken free and jumped into the sea. Swiftly she swam across the waves to the tiny island in the middle of the harbor. Pulling herself out of the water, she rose and faced the people on the pier.

Seeing her on the island and the boy beside the two elephants, the crowd began to clap. Soon the entire harbor was clapping.

"Long live the boy of the song!"

"Long live the girl of the sea!"

"Long live their friends, the elephants!"

The cheering only stopped when Little Fish's guardian stood on a box and asked for silence. "Merchant! Merchant!" she called. As the crowd pushed the thin man in front of her, she said, "Listen to me, merchant. Little Fish does not deserve a life in the Land of Sand. Have pity on her. Let her go."

The crowd cheered heartily. There were so many people cheering that the merchant could only bow his head. "And you," the old woman said, pointing to Diego Belloso. "Little Bird may be yours. The two elephants may be yours. But you cannot keep them unless Little Fish is also yours. They belong together. You must take them all with you."

Diego Belloso nodded.

As everyone watched and cheered, Little Bird, Little Fish, and the two elephants walked up the ramp into Diego Belloso's ship. Soon all were sailing together across the wild, dark sea toward the country of many islands called Filipinas.

What Is Serendipity?

by Twink Macaraig
Illustration by Beth A. Parrocha

Mica heard a word, a most wonderful word. It happened while Mica's parents were talking and they didn't realize that she was listening. Most of the time, Mica didn't bother to listen when grown-ups talked to each other. They used long words in flat, serious tones and rarely had anything exciting to say. But one evening Mica heard something so different from anything she'd heard before.

"He says here, the key to any great success is not just luck, but *serendipity,*" Mama was saying, as she was browsing through a shiny magazine. And as she said it, Mama's face looked the way it looked when she was describing how she used to play Chinese jackstones when she was a little girl or the *natilla* that Lola used to bake. Then the look was gone, Mama was her regular self again. Her grown-up conversation with Papa continued.

"Serendipity," Mica said softly to herself. "Ssehh-rehhenn—" she stretched out the sounds "—dpithy," she finished quickly, producing three little pops. *It's like a song,* she thought. Serendipity-doo-dah! Mama made it seem like such an important word, but it was so simple to say.

Mica didn't know what the word meant, but she liked the sound of it. She liked it very much, indeed. It sounded like something she would yell when Mama and Papa said that it was alright to yell as loud as she liked. Like the time she looked down the dark wishing well in the back of Lolo's house in the province. Instead of calling "Hello," she would shout "Serendipity!" and the echo would laugh back, "Tee-hee-hee."

It sounded like something she would say whenever she made an amazing discovery. Like the time she learned to cross her eyes and saw two of everything. Or that feeding a carabao wasn't anything to be scared of. The carabao ate the grass out of her hand, and its tongue was just a little wet, like her own.

She wanted to find serendipity so she could surprise her mother with some of it. Mama was looking very tired lately. But first, she had to find out what serendipity meant.

As Mica lay in bed, the word wouldn't stop repeating itself in her head. She asked her Yaya Paz, who was crocheting a blouse by her bedside, "Yaya, what is serendipity?"

Yaya Paz replied, after thinking awhile, "I think it's the name of a mischievous, little mermaid who likes to watch children build sand castles on the beach. When it gets dark, or the children have been playing too long, Serendipity blows the water to wash away the sand castles so the children know it's time to go. Then, tired from blowing so many waves, Serendipity goes home, deep in the ocean to her mother, who sings a song to send her to sleep."

As Yaya Paz hummed the lullaby that the mother mermaid sang, Mica figured that she was being tricked, but she didn't mind. She felt her eyelids growing heavy. But still her dreams were about serendipity. What in the world did it mean?

At breakfast the next morning Mica thought hard, *I haven't heard Mama use that word before, not Papa or Lolo, not even Teacher Marilyn. It must be something kept secret from little kids like me. Could it be a secret food,* she wondered, *that gave you powers like Popeye's spinach?*

She looked around her. It couldn't be the pork and beans. She ate it all the time. And it certainly couldn't be the *champorado.*

There was a clear bottle on the table containing bright strands of yellow, white, and orange and some tidbits of red. Papa ate this sometimes with his *tapa* or *longganisa,* but Mica had never tried it before. *It looks so tasty, but it has never been offered to me,* Mica realized, *not like the* kangkong *that Mama insists I eat. Could this be serendipity?*

But it didn't taste at all the way it looked, or so Mica thought at first. She imagined it would taste like the gaily colored candies that hang from the window of the *sari-sari* store. Or maybe like *pancit* because of the fine noodle-like shreds. But this stuff was kind of sweet, kind of sour, and kind of something else she couldn't describe. How could Papa eat this? She ate a little more, trying to figure out the taste. And slowly, bit by bit, she decided that it wasn't bad at all!

Mica was convinced that she had found the secret of

serendipity. This food that looked pretty, but tasted strange, but tasted good, but tasted different. *This is serendipity,* she decided, *or it tastes very much like it. This is the key to great success.* She couldn't wait to tell Mama when she got home.

But Mama wouldn't be back for a while, so Mica went to the park to play. It had been several days since she was last there because Mica had gotten tired of the same old jungle gym. But now everything—the sandbox, with the circus animals painted on the roof, the swings that squeaked, and the striped see-saws—looked fun once more.

"Serendipity!" she shrieked, as she whizzed down the slide. She went down so fast that she reached the bottom just as she finished the word.

"Serendipity!" she hollered every time she swung forward, using her toes to give herself a mighty push. With her eyes shut and her head tilted back, she could hear the wind rushing past her, as though murmuring a reply.

Then she felt something on her nose. Something so tiny and faint she might not have noticed it at all. It was a golden leaf from the giant *sampaloc* tree above. It was raining sampaloc leaves, and they were falling gracefully to the grass. Except for the one golden leaf that had found its way to Mica.

"This means I get a magic wish," Mica said to the sampaloc tree. "For every leaf I catch, I have a magic wish." Then, a new thought came into Mica's head. What if serendipity wasn't something to eat after all? What if it was right here on the tip of her finger? What if serendipity was this golden sampaloc leaf bearing Mica a magic wish?

"Of course! Of course!" Mica cried with delight, as she

kept the leaf carefully in her pocket. "The more serendipities I catch, the more wishes I get. Then I'll wish great success for Mama so that she won't be so tired anymore."

Mica watched for another shower. With the next breeze, she lifted her skirt to use as a net. Then she ran back and forth, turning and twirling, trying to be at the precise spot where each leaf was going to fall. It wasn't easy to do. There were far too many of them. And they were blowing about in all sorts of directions, making Mica miss a few. But Mica didn't give up. She waited breathlessly for each gust of wind to send down another shower of leaves and off she would go, clutching the edge of her skirt, catching as many serendipities as she could.

Pretty soon a little girl in pigtails was doing the same thing, joined by Mang Jun, who caught what he could with his *salakot*. Even the yayas, who had been chatting intently on the park bench, hoisted their aprons and joined in the merry scramble for falling wishes.

When Mica grew tired, and her neck ached from looking up too long, she counted her leaves. There were seventeen in her skirt...plus the first one in her pocket...that gave her eighteen serendipities in all. Mica ran home with the golden leaves in her fists, raised above her head, the way runners do when they cross the finish line first.

"Serendipity!" cried Mica as she burst into her bedroom. So thrilled was she over her catch that she bounced on her bed over and over again until she could almost, just almost, touch the ceiling.

I'd better keep these before they get lost, she remembered. She took her piggy bank down from the shelf and dropped the sampaloc leaves through the slot. One, two, three, four… she was getting to eleven when something caught her eye.

It was a little doll from many months before. It had come in a goodie bag from a cousin's birthday party. The doll was made entirely of cloth, her thick limbs stuffed with what felt like sand. She didn't bend or talk. Her eyes didn't close when you laid her down. In fact, her entire face was painted with only two colors: black for the eyes, lashes, brows, and nose; and pink for the cheeks and heart-shaped lips. When she first saw her, Mica didn't think that she was a very nice doll. She was too squat; she was hard to hug at night; and she just wasn't very pretty at all.

"She's not meant to be pretty. She's a pincushion," Yaya Paz had said then.

Mica couldn't imagine why she would ever want to stick pins into anything. So she lost herself instead in the bubble pipe, the floral stickers, and all the other delightful things that were in the goodie bag.

The doll was put on the shelf, propped on top of Mica's books, and was forgotten until Mica noticed her now.

She's been there so long, quietly waiting for me to care for her, Mica realized. She felt ashamed for all the games that she had played with all her other toys which the pincushion doll hadn't joined. Or the times that she couldn't find anything to do and didn't even think to take the doll from her perch.

"It's not your fault you're plain," consoled Mica, as she took the doll tenderly in her hands. The doll's dress had faded and her face had turned slightly gray from the dust. But her expression remained sweet and patient and wise.

"I bet you've been watching over me all this time, haven't

you? You've been guarding me at night when Yaya Paz says monsters and *mumu*s and white ladies can sneak in through the window. You've been protecting me from harm like an angel," Mica said.

The doll seemed to nod.

"I'm sorry, old doll," Mica whispered. "I'm sorry I didn't pay any attention to you."

The doll kept her cheery smile, and in her black-dot eyes Mica could see forgiveness.

"From now on, you'll join me and the others. You can help me fix Baby Rose's hair. You can cook rice with my mini rice cooker. You can even ride my magic pony." Mica was thinking of all the fun they would have together to make up for all the loneliness the doll must have felt during the many months that she had been ignored.

"And from now on, I will give you a proper name of your own, like all the other dolls. I will call you—" Mica knew that it could be nothing else but—"I will call you Serendipity."

Serendipity looked pleased and proud. Just then Mica heard a car drive up. "Mama!" Mica rushed to gather the day's treasures to present to her mother.

Mama looked up from the bills that she was sorting through. "So what did you do with yourself today?" she asked.

"Oh Mama, I have found the key to great success! I have found serendipity!" Mica announced grandly.

Mama looked closely at Mica's face, her eyebrows crinkled, as if she was trying to concentrate really hard. "What is serendipity, Mica?" she finally asked. "What do you think it is?"

"Yaya Paz said it was a little mermaid, but I think she was fooling me. I'm sure it's at least one of these things, Mama," she said, putting the jar she discovered at breakfast on the table. "It's this stuff that looks like candy pansit, but doesn't taste like it. It looks soft and wet, but has a tiny crunch when you bite it. It tastes weird at first, but after a while it's delicious. Try it, Mama. It'll give you super strength. Or it'll make you super successful. Then you won't look so tired anymore."

Mama stared at the bottle, but all she said was, "Hmm, most people call it *achara*, but it does taste interesting, come to think of it."

Mica emptied the contents of her piggy bank onto her mother's lap. "Or it's these golden leaves, Mama, from the big old sampaloc tree in the park. If you catch them before they fall to the ground you get a magic wish. I caught eighteen serendipities in my skirt today. You can have some, Mama, or you can have them all. I can always catch some more tomorrow."

Mama had that funny expression again, the one she has whenever she talks about Chinese jackstones or natilla.

"Maybe the wishes won't work unless I go and catch some myself," Mama said. "May I go with you next time?"

"What a great idea!" exclaimed Mica. "You can wear your swirly skirt with the flowers so you can catch lots of them. I'll wish for a baby brother and you can wish for great success…. But wait, I almost forgot…you have to meet my old new friend. This is Serendipity." Mica handed the doll to her mother.

"She's not very cute and she's a little worn. But she's sweet and loyal, and she never complains. If you make her your friend, she'll keep away evil spirits so that you'll find success for sure."

Mama was smiling broadly now.

"I call her Serendipity because she seems like one to me. Am I right, Mama? Or is serendipity the magic leaf? Or the candy-colored food? That's serendipity, isn't it?"

"You're absolutely right about all of them!" Mama burst into merry laughter. She swept Mica up into her arms and explained, "Serendipity is whatever you think it is, wherever you find it. When you feel joy in something that other people may overlook. When something makes you happy even though it doesn't seem all that important. When you find something special in something ordinary. When you find something by accident, that is serendipity."

Mica was thrilled that she had been right all along. Serendipity was everything she thought it was, as wonderful a word as it sounded. She hugged Mama tightly, then thought to ask again. "So would you like some more of my serendipity, Mama? Your magazine said it was the key to great success."

Mama stroked Mica's cheek. "I would love for you to share it with me all the time, Mica, not because the magazine said so, but because you have so much of it. And someday I want to be just as great a success as you are."

Mica felt a great warmth flow through her. She rubbed her face against Mama's dress to get as close as she possibly could and to smell the familiar jasmine scent Mama used. As her mother bent to kiss her forehead, Mica noticed that for the first time in a long, long time, Mama didn't look tired at all.

Pan de Sal Saves the Day

by Norma Olizon-Chikiamco
Illustration by Lyra Abueg Garcellano

Of all the kids in school, Pan de Sal felt she was the unluckiest. She didn't like the way she looked. Her skin was too dark, and she found her oblong shape weird. She also hated her rather flat nose. Besides, whoever heard of a girl named Pan de Sal anyway?

How she envied her classmates. There was Croissant, with her golden brown skin, tall nose, and curves in all the right places. And there was Danish, who looked so fair and neat, with beauty marks here and there that reminded Pan de Sal of sweet raisins. Muffin's skin was brown, too, but unlike Pan de Sal's, it glowed and made Muffin look so attractive. Many people in school liked Muffin because she was so sweet.

Some people thought Doughnut had a rather odd shape. But it didn't matter because he always impressed people with his rich wardrobe. Sometimes he came to school all in white, much like the frosting on a cake. At other times Doughnut wore chocolate-colored outfits or clothes the shade of strawberry milkshake.

Honey Bread was popular, too. Of course she got her name from her glossy complexion—which was exactly the same shade as honey. She often got into sticky situations, but since she was so cute, everybody forgave her. Her brother, Super Bread, was probably the fairest boy in class, so never mind that he was much too square. Besides, he always had all the right answers to everything. No wonder they called him Super. Their cousin, Bread Stick, was very tall and slim. She came all the way from Italy, and she was sure that she was going to be a famous fashion model some day.

All of Pan de Sal's classmates lived in beautiful houses. Croissant's parents had a lovely chalet on a hilltop, with a panoramic view of the countryside. Honey and Super Bread lived in a cozy cottage surrounded by a garden of roses, daisies, and sunflowers. All the rest had mansions, villas, or ranch-style homes, with luxurious furniture and all the modern appliances.

And Pan de Sal? *Poor me,* she thought every time she went home to the nipa hut she shared with her parents and younger brothers. Pan de Sal had to walk to and from school every day since they didn't have a car. At first her father walked with her to school, but when she learned the route, she had to go alone. After days of doing that, her legs no longer ached, and she even managed to find a shortcut.

Their nipa hut had bamboo slats for a floor and doors made of *sawali*. Sometimes the cold wind would blow through the flimsy walls. To keep warm, Pan de Sal and her brothers would huddle under the blankets that their grandmother had woven for them.

Pan de Sal also did her share of the house chores. She washed all the dishes with water that her father fetched from a nearby well. To polish the floor, she and her mother used large leaves, which removed all the dirt and made the floor look shiny and bright.

They had no television, so for entertainment Pan de Sal and her brothers would sing. Their mother taught them all the songs she had learned as a child, and the family would often gather after supper to hear her sing of immortal love, of the happy life in the countryside, and of an old pair of wooden shoes.

Pan de Sal inherited her mother's lovely voice. In school, music was her favorite subject and she would have joined the Glee Club had she not been too shy to audition.

Pan de Sal and her brothers didn't have expensive toys, so instead they made up their own games. They loved running in the open fields surrounding their nipa hut, climbing up trees, and playing *sipa*. Pan de Sal and her brothers had different kinds of sipa, which they had made out of old newspapers or brown paper bags. Pan de Sal's favorite sipa was pink and white. She had made it out of paper buntings left over from a town fiesta. Often when they finished their chores early, Pan de Sal and her brothers would play sipa. She became so good at it that she could kick it up in the air a hundred times without letting it touch the ground.

One day the class went on a field trip with their teacher, Miss Floures. The school driver, Mang Baking, drove them to a nature park where they could learn about trees, flowers, and insects. They saw all kinds of fruit trees like mango and star apple, flowering plants like jasmine and *sampaguita,* as well as colorful dragonflies, butterflies, ladybugs, and grasshoppers. Pan de Sal was familiar with most of these creatures because they were plentiful in the fields where she and her brothers played on weekends.

"Eeeek!" Croissant shrieked when an insect landed on her.

"Don't be afraid," Pan de Sal said. "It's only a dragonfly. Look, I can even catch it, and it won't bite." Pan de Sal closed her thumb and forefinger on the dragonfly's wings and held it up for Croissant to see.

"Gross!" Croissant said as she looked away, but by this time Super Bread and Doughnut had joined them and were fascinated by the dragonfly.

"Wow, you're brave," said Super Bread, and Pan de Sal felt strangely proud of herself, though it was really no big deal. Why, one time she had even caught a whole army of dragonflies, which she had shown her brothers before setting the insects free.

When it was time for lunch they all sat down on the picnic grounds and opened their lunch boxes. Out came hamburgers and french fries, spaghetti, fried chicken, and pizza, all neatly wrapped in aluminum foil. Croissant even had a cheese soufflé, while Bread Stick brought fettucine with cream sauce.

Suddenly Pan de Sal felt ashamed of her brown paper bag. In it she had rice, broiled fish with tomatoes and onions, and chicken *adobo,* all wrapped in banana leaves. Her mother had made sure Pan de Sal brought plenty of food so she could share it with her classmates, and her brothers had slipped in some bananas, which they had picked from the tree in their back yard. Pan de Sal loved her food but compared to that of her classmates, the rice, fish, adobo, and bananas suddenly looked so…humble.

"Haven't you brought anything to eat?" Miss Floures asked Pan de Sal.

"Uh, I forgot my *baon*," she lied.

"Oh, but you must eat or you'll be hungry. Here, have some of my barbecue." Miss Floures gave her slices of charcoal-broiled pork on bamboo skewers.

"Have some fettucine," Bread Stick offered. "And some fried chicken," said Doughnut.

Soon everyone was sharing their baon with her. Pan de Sal felt grateful and sad at the same time. If only she could share her food with her classmates, too.

When lunch was over, the children piled into the bus and Mang Baking got into the driver's seat to take them back to school. They had driven only a few kilometers when suddenly the bus stopped. Mang Baking got out and looked at the engine. But he could not figure out what was wrong. They were on a lonely country road with no house in sight. Finally he decided to go for help. "Stay here while I look for the nearest gas station," Mang Baking told Miss Floures and the children.

At first they all sat still but before long, everyone grew restless. "Mang Baking sure is taking a long, long time," Danish said.

"I'm bored," complained Honey Bread. "I wish there was something we could do."

"Why don't we play a game?" Miss Floures suggested.

"But what will we play?" Honey Bread asked. "We didn't bring our computer games."

"And I forgot my Frisbee," Doughnut said.

"I have my sipa!" Pan de Sal suddenly volunteered.

"Sipa?!" everyone turned to look at her. "What in the world is that?"

"Uh, it's a…little toy." Pan de Sal suddenly wished she hadn't spoken.

"Well, show it to us," said Miss Floures, "so we can learn how to play with it, too."

Pan de Sal fished the sipa out of her pocket. It was her favorite sipa, the pink-and-white one made from leftover paper buntings.

"Far out!" said Doughnut. "But what do you do with it?"

Everyone got out of the bus so Pan de Sal could show them. She kicked the sipa up in the air, once, twice, and several more times until she reached the count of twenty.

"Wow, that's totally rad!" said Muffin. "Can I try, too?"

Soon everyone was having fun playing with the sipa. "This sure is a great game!" Bread Stick said.

"And it's good exercise, too," Super Bread pointed out.

Even Miss Floures tried the sipa a few times and laughed when she reached only a score of ten. But everyone marveled when Pan de Sal kicked it up in the air all of a hundred times.

"Wow! You sure are great at playing sipa," Bread Stick said.

"I've had a lot of practice," Pan de Sal explained, remembering all those times she and her brothers played sipa on weekends.

After the game, everyone was hungry again. But they had all finished their lunches and had nothing left to eat. Pan de Sal spoke up once more. "I have some food in my paper bag if you want it," she offered shyly.

"Well, take it out so we can all share it," Miss Floures said.

Pan de Sal peeled back the banana leaves and spread out the rice, broiled fish, and adobo.

"Hey, this is yummy!" said Doughnut, as he spooned in a bit of adobo and some rice. "I've never tasted such great food in my life."

The others also loved the broiled fish and feasted on the sweet bananas. "Fresh fruit is good for your health," Super Bread told everyone between mouthfuls of food.

"Why didn't you tell us you had brought some food?" Miss Floures asked Pan de Sal.

"I was too ashamed," Pan de Sal admitted. "I thought you might find my food yucky."

"Are you kidding?" Croissant said. "This is a great change from all the soufflés, quiches, and bisques that we have at home. You should give us the recipes."

Pan de Sal glowed. How wonderful to be able to share something with her classmates.

After they had eaten, the children sat cozily in their seats to rest and wait for Mang Baking.

"Who wants to sing?" Miss Floures asked.

"Not me," Honey Bread croaked. "I almost flunked music."

"Don't look at me," Super Bread said. "I'd rather play Scrabble."

"Perhaps Pan de Sal can sing," suggested Muffin. "I heard her humming once in school."

Soon Pan de Sal was singing a *kundiman*.

"*Dahil sa iyo…Nais kong mabuhay,*" she began. "*Dahil sa iyo, hanggang mamatay…Dapat mong tantuin, wala nang ibang giliw…Puso ko'y tanungin, ikaw at ikaw rin…*"

Pan de Sal sang all the songs her mother taught her.

"*Maalaala mo kaya…ang sumpa mo sa akin…Na ang pag-ibig mo ay sadyang di magmamaliw…Kung nais mong matanto…Buksan ang aking puso…At doo'y larawan mo ang tanging nakatago…*

"*Leron, Leron sinta, umakyat sa papaya…Dala-dala'y buslo, sisidlan ng bunga…*

"*Ikaw ang aking panaginip…Ikaw ang tibok ng dibdib…*

"*Bakya mo, Neneng, luma at kupas na…Nguni't may bakas pa ng luha mo, Sinta…*

"*Sa kabukiran, walang kalungkutan…Lahat ng araw ayyyyy…Kaligayahan…*"

The children were amused and amazed at Pan de Sal's songs. They had no idea that their classmate, who hardly spoke a word to anyone, was so talented. They clapped after every song and sat on the edge of their seats so they could hear Pan de Sal better. Before long, her beautiful voice lulled them into sweet slumber.

"Pan de Sal, you sing so well. You should join the Glee Club," Miss Floures whispered. "On Monday I'll accompany you to Miss Kanta personally and tell her what a great voice you have."

"Oh, thank you, Miss Floures," said Pan de Sal. "I've

always wanted to join the Glee Club. But I was too shy to try out."

"Nonsense," said Miss Floures. "When you have talent, you shouldn't be afraid to share it. By using your talent properly, you can make many people happy."

Soon Mang Baking arrived with a mechanic. They poked and tapped the engine, and finally the bus hummed back to life. They were on their way back to school.

"Pan de Sal, you saved the day!" Miss Floures said as they got down from the bus. "You've taught us a game, fed us delicious food, and sang many beautiful songs. You're one of the best students in class!"

"That's for sure!" Bread Stick, Croissant, and Honey Bread chorused.

"You're all rrrrright!" the others exclaimed.

That afternoon Pan de Sal rushed to their nipa hut, her heart pounding with happiness and joy. She no longer felt like the odd one out at school. She felt unique, a person like no other, with her own special talents and abilities. And she would finally join the Glee Club!

"Hmmmmm. Maybe I like the name Pan de Sal after all," she told herself as she helped her mother prepare supper.

PURE MAGIC

by Lakambini A. Sitoy
Illustration by Brian Uhing

Each day Ellen would peer out the window to see if Mirava was coming up the street. Mirava lived three blocks away and was older by a year, but come summer they always played together at the house where Ellen lived with her grandmother. It was big and old, full of musty furniture and faded, brown family portraits. Outside there was lots of yard to romp in. The shrubbery was so overgrown the two girls could sit under a bush at high noon and feel none of the summer sun.

It was a house full of secrets. In a cupboard was a bracelet made out of a bent silver fork. Underneath Ellen's bed, caught between two of the floorboards, was the yellowed fragment of a letter. That dress the color of shrivelled cobwebs hanging in the corner of Lola Lagring's wardrobe—that dress had once been yards and yards of rose-colored lace. Lola Lagring had worn it more than half a century ago at her coming-out party.

In the dining room behind one of the *narra* panels there was a hidden passage. "There's a door in your wall," Mirava said one day, staring intently at the woodwork. They passed their hands over the panelling. And there it was, a tiny knob. Gently, the two girls tugged at it, taking turns, until the panel gave. It *was* a door, just big enough for each one to crawl through on her hands and knees. It had been cemented shut by tiny cobwebs. Behind it was a tunnel with only blackness at the far end.

But not all the secrets were dark and old: the vine, for instance, growing wild across the garden's east wall. One morning Ellen tracked its path, ruffling through the leaves until she came across a brown shrivelled something. She was about to toss it away when it popped open—a ripe pod, and half a dozen precious seeds, bright red with ebony eyes, rolled into her palm.

And the cave, that was another secret: an empty space in the middle of the stand of umbrella palms near the old forgotten carp pool. A latticework of stalks formed the walls, and vines of purple morning glory grew among the leaves of the palms, which were like the ribs of little umbrellas.

In the cave, listening to Mirava, Ellen forgot that she was just a little girl living with her grandmother in a big dark house. Mirava could do magic. She'd take the bright red seeds with their little, beady eyes, and cup them in her palm. In her hands they were more than seeds. They were witch's jewels, and running her fingers through them Mirava would tell stories of the house and the garden.

That scrap of paper Ellen had found under her bed— that had come, said Mirava, from a letter sent by Lola

Lagring's first fiancé, a long time ago. He had written her to say he was marrying someone else. Lola Lagring had torn up the letter and in a rage, had clasped her hands around the fork so tightly that blue sparks flew and the utensil bent upon itself until it looked like a delicate silver shackle.

"And what happened to the man?" Ellen whispered.

Mirava thought hard for a moment. "Oh, but he's still here, in your house," she said. "At the end of that tunnel in your dining room is a little chamber, and he sleeps there, as handsome as he was the day your lola popped him in fifty years ago. And then she went and married your grandfather, knowing if he did her wrong, her beloved would still be there waiting patiently for her."

"I don't believe you," Ellen said, but nonetheless she shivered. Was her lola a witch? Was Mirava? What if what she said was true? Was there really a handsome young man sleeping only a few feet from where she and her lola had their *tapa* and rice every morning? What would it be like to sneak into the secret passage when Lola Lagring wasn't looking?

She knew very well she'd probably just end up in some gray storage chamber filled with things too ruined and ugly to put around the house. But what if she believed, really believed Mirava's little tale? Would the strength of their believing make it somehow come true?

But it was hard to keep believing when no one else did. From time to time Ellen's parents called her long distance.

"Have you made any new friends?" her mother would say. Her mother, who was in Manila, worried about Mirava. "I'm not sure how anyone who makes up stories about other people is a good influence," she said once.

Her father's calls were from San Francisco. "Are you studying hard, Ellen?" he said, even though it was the middle of summer. He was deathly afraid that she would repeat a grade.

"When are you coming home?" Ellen would say into the black receiver. "Will you both come and live with me when you're back?" But neither of them replied to that.

Mirava didn't have a spell to bring parents back, or even make them believe in magic.

"Too hard," she said. "I'm only a junior witch. Think of something different."

So Ellen would think and think, and with the strength of her thoughts, what her parents said or did somehow grew less important than the cave and the shrubbery and the secrets of the big old house.

One afternoon the two girls were lying in the grass, gazing up at the star apple tree, at the brown undersides of its leaves. They both loved star apples, but it was too late in the year for them; there had been no fruits since March, when the last of the harvest had shrivelled up and dropped from the branches. But Mirava was trying to make the little fruits grow. She clutched the red-and-black wishing seeds and mumbled a rhyme to herself, over and over. But as she murmured the spell, a change came over the day. The sunlight turned sickly. It was straggling through the kind of clouds they had not seen for months.

Ellen sat up. "It's going to rain."

Mirava took no notice.

"It's summer, and it's going to rain!" Ellen wailed.

Gracia, the maid, in the garden sweeping leaves, heard her. "That's because summer's almost over," she said. "Soon you'll be going off to school again."

Panic clutched at Ellen. School! She'd forgotten all about school. "Gracia, when does school start?"

"Well, I think, in June."

"When's June?"

And Gracia began to count on her fingers: one, two, three, four....

Ellen groaned. Summer's end was only two weeks away.

Why, everything would change once she and Mirava were back in school! They wouldn't have time to sit in the umbrella-palm cave every afternoon. They couldn't even play together at recess. Mirava was one grade ahead, and her friends would laugh at Ellen. They'd tell her to run along, to get lost.

And it would rain. The start of school meant rain, rain, and more rain. When she was little she and her mother played in the warm, warm rain, but then her father had gotten mad. Whenever she thought about her parents they were always yelling and storming over the sound of the rain.

"Mirava, make the rain go away!" she said suddenly.

Mirava turned to her and she could see that she was thinking the exact same thing. But then she frowned. "I've never done it before."

"It's no big deal!" Ellen replied in a rush. "Come on, we'll do it together. We don't need anything special—we'll just *wish*."

They knew they would have to wait until the very moment the rain fell to earth. But it took its own pretty time. For days the clouds gathered and retreated, gathered and retreated, gathered, until at last the rain came, a curtain of warm needles that grew bigger and bigger and fell faster and faster, marching through the streets and in their garden.

"Quick, quick, send it away!" Mirava shrieked, and they both ran out into the garden, stomping through the dry, crushed grass, waving their arms and hollering, laughing their throats hoarse. They danced until the water got too cold to bear, and even went on for a few more minutes for good measure, stopping only when Gracia stumbled out with an umbrella and hauled in the two of them.

"Do you think that was good enough?" Ellen said.

Mirava sneezed. "I think so." And then she sneezed again.

The next day Mirava didn't visit. She had run the three blocks to her house in the wind and rain, and come down with a fever. Ellen, whom Gracia had bundled off in a towel straight into the hot tub, was fine. But she moped around, mad at her friend for getting sick. Several days passed, but Mirava was still ill. They went over for a visit—Gracia and Lola Lagring and Ellen—and Ellen wanted to linger in the room where Mirava lay in semi-darkness, her face pale yellow against the pillow. But Lola Lagring jerked her back sharply and pushed her out. Lola and the sick girl's mother whispered for quite a while. Then Lola Lagring drew Ellen aside. "Mirava is very, very ill," she said. "Let's hope her lungs won't give up. You must help me pray."

Ellen sat for a long time in her room after that. Was Mirava going to die? Lola said extra prayers only for the dead. She couldn't imagine what it would be like if her friend

were gone. Something like the empty way she felt now, perhaps, only worse, because it would go on forever.

She needed something to do. She looked under the bed. Surely there were more fragments of old paper wedged between the floorboards. How pleased Mirava would be when she got back to find that Ellen had pieced together the whole of the letter from her grandmother's fiancé. But the boards were bare.

She wandered through the silent house. The secret passage—she would ask Gracia to open it up and look all the way in. She went to the dining room. But the panelling was perfectly smooth. Try as she might she couldn't find the knob that marked the secret door.

Ellen opened drawer after drawer, searching for the silver bracelet made out of a fork. But it was gone.

Something was wrong. Something was very wrong. She ran breathlessly out to the garden. *Witch's jewels*, she thought. *I need some witch's jewels.* But the vine along the east wall where she had found the seeds was gone, too. She searched and searched. Had Gracia torn it loose? But there was no sign of disturbance in the foliage. It had simply disappeared.

She sat down in the mud, her heart pounding. Without Mirava none of the secrets of the big old house and the garden were real. *I need some magic*, she thought. *Some magic to bring them back.* But she knew she couldn't do it all on her own. All by herself she wasn't that powerful. She needed Mirava. And Mirava was ill. But that was it, she thought. Mirava she *could* bring back. And she knew just how to do it.

Ellen scoured the garden and the house for what she needed. When Lola Lagring was at her siesta she slipped out the gate, ventured into the streets and as far up as the river and as far down as the seashore and around the rocky walls of the ancient church in the town. She knew she had no time to lose. As she ran lightly over the newly-wet earth the picture of Mirava's face, deathly pale against the pillow, rose up again and again in her mind.

And late one afternoon several days later she knew she had all she needed. She bundled everything up in a hanky and sped through the gathering dusk to Mirava's house, entering without knocking, bursting into her friend's room.

"Ellen?" Mirava said, raising herself up on one elbow. Her face looked pale and sharp in the half-light.

"You must get well!" Ellen cried. "I-can't-get-into-the-cave-anymore-and-I-can't-find-the-secret-door-they're-all-gone-and-you-can't-be-sick-you-musn't-be-sick...." She broke off and fumbled for her knotted handkerchief, crying out, "Look what I brought you!" as she emptied the contents of the hanky onto the blanket that half-covered Mirava.

Fern fossils etched into little, white rocks, strange, round shells called cat's eyes, old coins, and shards of green glass worn smooth by the tides. Scarlet-and-ebony seeds and pretty beach stones, a blue kingfisher feather, dried flowers, and bits of fishbone. Things that throbbed with old magic, with the pure, old magic of summer, which she now spread triumphantly over the sheet. The corners of her friend's mouth quivered.

"They're beautiful," Mirava murmured. She raised herself ever so slowly up on one elbow to stare at the treasures. Gingerly she picked up the feather and a moonstone and held them against her ear.

"How do I look?" she whispered, and she looked so funny, so much like a little shaman, so much like the old healthy Mirava that Ellen couldn't suppress the laughter that welled up from deep inside her. Mirava managed a weak grin, and then a chuckle that sounded at first like a cough.

"You're not sick. You can't be sick!" Ellen cried out with such exuberance that Mirava finally laughed out loud, and her mother came puzzled to the door to see what was going on. Peeking around the corner of the door she was dumbfounded to see the two little girls laughing and chattering as they lined the precious summer jewels up on the white sheet, forming birds on the wing and curled up kittens and the five points of a star.

Later that night Gracia came over and carried Ellen, half-asleep but happy, back to their own home. "What have you done this time, you bad girl," she muttered, but only half chidingly. Mirava was sleeping soundly, her color mostly back, her fever all gone.

"A miracle," she and Lola Lagring murmured.

Ellen, nodding off over dinner, only smiled. "No, not a miracle," she said to herself. "Magic.

"You see, Lola," she said to her grandmother. "I can be a junior witch, too."

The old woman only smiled. She didn't understand.

Ellen slid out of her seat and went to the window. The garden was all wet from the rain and bathed in silver rays from the rising moon. She yawned. In a few days, when Mirava was all better, they would search for the silver bracelet and the secret passage and the vine with the red-and-black witch's eyes. And if they didn't find them then it was all right, still. Summer was ending, perhaps, but time passed swiftly, ever so swiftly—wasn't that what her lola was fond of saying? The important thing was that Mirava was back. There would be other summers and new secrets for old— and magic, fresh magic.

About the Authors

Marivi Soliven Blanco ("Chun," Second Prize, 1992 Don Carlos Palanca Memorial Awards for Literature) earned a master's degree in teaching from Simmons College in Boston, U.S.A. She received her bachelor's degree in mass communications *magna cum laude* from the University of the Philippines. Ms. Blanco is the author of *The Unicorn, The Toad and the Princess, Philippine Fright: 13 Scary Stories, Chief Flower Girl,* as well as all the books in the *Jenny and Jay Pinoy Private Eyes* series.

Norma Olizon-Chikiamco ("Pan de Sal Saves the Day," First Prize, 1995 Don Carlos Palanca Memorial Awards for Literature) graduated with a bachelor's degree in journalism from St. Theresa's College. She is currently editor in chief of *Food Magazine* and a former editor of *Sunday Globe Magazine, Metro Magazine,* and *Celebrity Magazine.*

Leoncio P. Deriada ("The Man Who Hated Birds," First Prize, 1993 Don Carlos Palanca Memorial Awards for Literature) has a doctorate in English literature from Silliman University, a master's degree in English from Xavier University, and a bachelor's degree in English *cum laude* from Ateneo de Davao University. Dr. Deriada is the award-winning author of *The Road to Mawab and Other Stories, The Dog Eaters and Other Plays, Night Mares,* and *The Week of the Whales.*

Lina B. Diaz de Rivera ("The Gem," Second Prize, 1996 Don Carlos Palanca Memorial Awards for Literature) received her doctorate in English and her master's degree in reading from the University of the Philippines and her bachelor's degree in English from Far Eastern University. Dr. Diaz de Rivera is the author of the textbooks *Ferry in the Sun, Golden Galleon,* and *English for High School.*

Angelo Rodriguez Lacuesta ("The Daughter of the Wind," Third Prize, 1996 Don Carlos Palanca Memorial Awards for Literature) graduated with a bachelor's degree in biology from the University of the Philippines. His work has been published in *Likhaan Anthology of Poetry and Fiction, Gaudeamus/Caracoa, The Evening Paper, The Philippine Daily Inquirer, Sunday Inquirer Magazine, Philippine Graphic,* and *Philippines Free Press.*

Twink Macaraig ("What Is Serendipity?," First Prize, 1994 Don Carlos Palanca Memorial Awards for Literature) is pursuing graduate studies in business administration at the Singapore Institute of Management. She received her bachelor's degree in mass communications from the University of the Philippines. Ms. Macaraig is the author of *The Ultimate, Absolutely Indispensable Guide to Food Delivery in Metro Manila*. She is currently a news anchor for Asia Business News in Singapore.

Ino M. Manalo ("Little Bird, Little Fish, and the Two Elephants," Third Prize, 1993 Don Carlos Palanca Memorial Awards for Literature) graduated with a bachelor's degree in humanities from the University of the Philippines and a master's degree in international affairs from Columbia University. He is the author of *The Architect's Design* and *Botong: Alay at Alaala*.

Carla M. Pacis ("The Dream Weavers," Second Prize, 1995 Don Carlos Palanca Memorial Awards for Literature) received her master's degree in creative writing from the University of the Philippines and her bachelor's degree in economics from Assumption College. Ms. Pacis is the author of *There's a Snake in the House, All From the Same Tree*, and *Owl Friends*. She also edited *Water in the Ring of Fire*, a collection of folk tales.

Maria Elena Paterno ("The Blanket," First Prize, 1991 Don Carlos Palanca Memorial Awards for Literature) received her master's degree in education from Harvard University and her bachelor's degree in English and comparative literature from the University of the Philippines. Ms. Paterno is the award-winning author of two folk tale collections and a number of science books, including the 1994 National Book Awardee, *Earthquake!*

Lakambini A. Sitoy ("Pure Magic," First Prize, 1996 Don Carlos Palanca Memorial Awards for Literature) graduated with a bachelor's degree in biology from Silliman University. Her work has appeared in *The Evening Paper, Today*, and *Preview*.

ABOUT THE ARTISTS

Hermès Alègrè received his bachelor's degree in fine arts from Philippine Women's University. He is the illustrator of *Bahay Kubo* and *The Mats*, which won the 1995 National Book Award for Best Children's Literature. Mr. Alègrè's work has appeared in over 30 gallery exhibitions. He lives in Los Baños, Laguna.

Robert A. Alejandro is a children's book illustrator and designer with a bachelor's degree in fine arts from the University of the Philipines. He has illustrated two picture books, *Chief Flower Girl* and *The Unicorn*. In 1995 he won a National Book Award for Best Design for *A Field Guide to Whales and Dolphins in the Philippines*. He is a member of Ang Ilustrador ng Kabataan (INK) and lives in Quezon City.

Joanne de León graduated from the University of the Philippines with a bachelor's degree in fine arts. Her book *Ang Nawawalang Araw* won a prize at the 1992 Noma Concours for Picture Book Illustrations contest. She is the illustrator of *The Environmental Alphabet, Pinatubo, the Planted Mountain*, and two folk tale collections. Ms. de León is a member of Ang Ilustrador ng Kabataan (INK). She lives in Quezon City.

Albert Gamos has won numerous awards in the field of children's book illustration. In 1992 he was recognized by the Philippine Board on Books for Young People for his outstanding achievement in book illustration and design. A graduate of the University of the East School of Music and Arts, he is the illustrator of *A Child's Treasury of Philippine Christmas Stories* and *The Best of Lola Basyang: Timeless Tales for the Filipino Family*. He lives in Angeles City, Pampanga.

Lyra Abueg Garcellano is currently pursuing a second bachelor's degree, in fine arts, at the University of the Philippines. She has a bachelor's degree in interdisciplinary studies from the Ateneo de Manila University. Ms. Garcellano is the illustrator of *Philippine Pictionary: My First 100 Words* and *The Legend of Crying Mountain*. She is a member of Ang Ilustrador ng Kabataan (INK) and lives in Quezon City.

Felix Mago Miguel graduated *cum laude* from the University of the Philippines with a bachelor's degree in fine arts. Mr. Miguel was a semi-finalist at the 1992 and 1990 Metrobank National Painting competitions. Among the books he's illustrated are *Kablay, Alpabeto ng Rebolusyon, Matandang, Matabang Pusa*, and *Why the Piña Has a*

Hundred Eyes and Other Classic Philippine Folk Tales About Fruits. He is a member of Ang Ilustrador ng Kabataan (INK). He lives in Quezon City.

Arnel Mirasol studied fine arts at the University of Sto. Tomas and the University of the East. He was a grand prize co-winner of the 1984 Metrobank Painting Competition and a finalist for the 1995 Illustrator's Prize of the Philippine Board on Books for Young People. Mr. Mirasol is the illustrator of *Tamales Day!* He is also a textbook illustrator and political cartoonist. He lives in Tondo, Manila.

Beth A. Parrocha graduated with a bachelor's degree in fine arts from the University of the Philippines. She illustrated *The First Cashew Nut, I Can Do It Myself,* and *The Boy Who Ate Stars.* She designed *Philippine Picture Postcards,* which won the 1994 National Book Award for Best Design. Ms. Parrocha is a member of Ang Ilustrador ng Kabataan (INK). She lives in Parañaque, Metro Manila.

Brian Uhing studied fine arts at the University of the Philippines. He received two awards at the Lion's Club Art Contest. A painter and muralist by trade, this is his first venture into children's book illustration. Mr. Uhing lives in Antipolo, Rizal.

Auri Asuncion Yambao received her bachelor's degree in fine arts *cum laude* from the University of the Philippines. In 1989 she received the Best Illustration Award from the Creative Guild of the Philippines. Her illustrations have appeared in the *Himig* series and *Mabuhay* magazine. She lives in Quezon City.